KIDDING AROUND

San Diego

A YOUNG PERSON'S GUIDE TO THE CITY

RUTH J. LUHRS

ILLUSTRATED BY MARY LAMBERT

John Muir Publications
Santa Fe, New Mexico

For my sisters, Helen McElwain and Gloria Danna

With special thanks to Van, my husband and traveling companion, and to Sheila Berg, my editor

John Muir Publications, P.O. Box 613, Santa Fe, NM 87504

© 1991 by Ruth J. Luhrs
Illustrations © 1991 by Mary Lambert
Cover © 1991 by John Muir Publications
All rights reserved. Published 1991
Printed in the United States of America

First edition. First printing September 1991.

Library of Congress Cataloging-in-Publication Data
Luhrs, Ruth J.
    Kidding around San Diego : a young person's guide to the city / Ruth J. Luhrs ; illustrated by Mary Lambert. — 1st ed.
      p. cm.
    Summary: A guide to the culture and interesting sights of San Diego and the surrounding area.
    ISBN 1-56261-010-4
    1. San Diego (Calif.)—Description—Guide-books—Juvenile literature. 2. Children—Travel—California—San Diego—Guide-books—Juvenile literature. [1. San Diego (Calif.)—Description—Guides.] I. Lambert, Mary, ill. II. Title.
F869.S22L84   1991
917.94'9850453—dc20   91-17169
                                                          CIP
                                                            AC

Designer: Joanna V. Hill
Typeface: Trump Medieval
Typesetter: Copygraphics, Inc., Santa Fe, New Mexico
Printer: Guynes Printing Company of New Mexico

Distributed to the book trade by
W. W. Norton & Company, Inc.
New York, New York

Contents

1. Anchors Aweigh / 4
2. "The City Beautiful" and How It Grew / 6
3. All Around the Town / 9
4. Getting in the Swim / 16
5. Mission Bay Park and Sea World / 21
6. Yachts and Yachts of Ships and Boats / 26
7. Past, Present, and Future / 31
8. Who's for the Zoo? / 38
9. Grease Paint, Galleries, and Glitz / 45
10. Cabrillo, Coronado, and Chula Vista / 48
11. South of the Border and the Backcountry / 54
12. Memories / 60
Appendix / 61

1. Anchors Aweigh

Meteorologists (those who study the weather) agree that San Diego has an ideal year-round climate. A typical day is sunny and mild with low humidity.

It's vacation time, and you couldn't find a more fun-filled place to visit than San Diego! And the weather is great—just one beautiful day after another.

What would you like to do? Explore a tide pool? Try surfing? See a killer whale perform, or pet a dolphin? Check out over fifty hands-on exhibits at a science center, or tour the town on a Molly Trolley? There is all this and much, much more. So bone up, and make a priority list of the things you want to do. On-the-spot plan changes are okay, too. That's part of the fun and adventure of traveling.

Now is the time to think about what you will need on the trip. Helter-skelter last-minute packing can lead to trouble: you could end up with earmuffs instead of swimwear. Travel light. Don't take more than you really need. Remember, at one time or another, you may have to carry everything you bring.

San Diegans are outdoor people. Jeans and shorts go most places, although you may want some nicer things for evenings out. Nights are usually cool any time of year. Bring a sweater or windbreaker—one with a hood is handy. It's apt to be breezy near the ocean.

Laundry? No problem. Even cottons dry quickly in this sunny climate. Bring along some sort of travel clothesline. Hotel people will appreciate a drip catcher to protect the floor. A plastic garbage bag will do the job, and it can also be used to carry wet swimsuits.

Comfortable walking shoes are a must. Bring thongs or old sneakers if you plan to snorkel or explore tide pools; rocks are hard on the feet.

All kinds of sports equipment can be rented—from bikes to boogie boards. If whale watching or bird-watching is on your list of things to do, you will need binoculars. They'll also come in handy for a close-up look at big navy ships and small boats, too. And don't forget your camera! Half the fun is remembering your vacation and showing pictures to friends.

Most everyone likes to send postcards. There are beautiful ones and funny ones in shops everywhere. But have you tried to find a post office when you are traveling? They always seem to be on the other side of town or on a one-way street going the other way. Why not buy stamps before you leave home and tuck them in with your address book?

Now you are ready for a really super vacation. Anchors aweigh and smooth sailing.

San Diego County covers 4,000 square miles. It is bordered on the west by the Pacific Ocean, on the east by mountains and Anza-Borrego Desert State Park, on the south by Mexico, and on the north by sprawling Los Angeles.

2. "The City Beautiful" and How It Grew

Around 4000 B.C.—The first San Diegans are prehistoric shell gatherers called La Jollans.

1000 B.C. (more or less)—Kumeyaay Indians from the desert country oust the La Jollans. The Kumeyaay weave watertight baskets, make pottery, and grind acorns.

A.D. 1542—The search for treasure and a passage to the Atlantic draws the Portuguese explorer, Juan Rodríguez Cabrillo into San Diego Bay, which he names San Miguel.

1602—Pirates are getting out of hand in the Pacific, so Spain decides to have another look at the safe harbors charted by Cabrillo. Sebastián Vizcaino is sent from Mexico to check them out. He renames San Miguel San Diego.

1769—Padre Junípero Serra joins a Spanish expedition to settle California. The padre thinks a chain of rest stops would be a good idea. He builds the first of his 21 missions, San Diego de Alcala, here.

1821—In Mexico, revolution against Spain simmers and boils over. When news of the Mexican war and independence reach the garrison on San Diego's Presidio Hill, the soldiers cut off their ribbon-tied queues, which marks them as king's men. (These may have been the first queue cuts.)

1833—Mexico confiscates mission holdings. Huge ranchos are founded on Mexican land grants. San Diego grows to a community of 400, not counting Indians.

1847—The Mexican-American war is declared, and conquest of California is peaceful—at first. General Kearny's army marches into big trouble near San Diego's San Pasqual Valley, where Andrís Pico's *Californios* are waiting for them. After a disastrous engagement, the Americans dig in. They are forced to eat their mules to survive. Kit Carson and two other men head for San Diego and return with 215 soldiers just in time to save the day.

September 9, 1850—California becomes the 31st state, with the bear flag as its symbol.

1869—Alonzo Horton sees little future for San Diego where it is located. He purchases 960 acres of mud flats for 27½ cents an acre and literally moves the town from the dry, dusty hills down to the shore. Three thousand people call San Diego home when gold is discovered in nearby Julian the same year.

1888—Rabbit hunters conceive the idea to build a resort hotel on Coronado Island. Hotel del Coronado (the Del) is soon open for business. Wyatt Earp is king of the rowdy waterfront district called Stingaree. He and his gambling halls are made unwelcome by most of San Diego's 16,000 people.

1898—The rusting post-Civil War gunboat USS *Pinta* becomes the first navy ship to call San Diego home port.

1914-1917—World War I. The navy takes to the air with the Curtiss A-1 Triad. This astounding new plane can land on water.

1915-1916—To celebrate the opening of the Panama Canal, San Diego holds the Panama-California Exposition. Doctors Harry and Paul Wegeforth round up animals left from the Exposition to start the San Diego Zoo.

1935—A new electronic device is exhibited at the California-Pacific Exposition. Some critics call the thing a gadget of little use. We call it TV.

1941—San Diego gets ready for war. Barrage balloons float overhead, and the bay is protected with submarine nets. The huge Rancho Santa Margarita near Oceanside is converted into the marines' Camp Pendleton.

1945—San Diego celebrates VJ Day and the war's end with an around-the-clock party. Mission Bay is dredged to make San Diego the aquatic center of the West Coast.

1964—Sea World opens with a splash—two shows and one aquarium.

1969—Ferryboats at work since the turn of the century give their last toot with the opening of the Coronado Bay Bridge.

1990—With a population of over one million, San Diego's need for more fresh water is growing. Supply, conservation, and rationing may be the most important problems faced in this decade.

3. All Around the Town

*As soon as you arrive in San Diego, get a free copy of "Arts, Activities, and Attractions" from the **International Visitor Information Center** (1st Ave. and F St., 11 Horton Plaza). It lists everything that's's going on in town—from sports to theater to museums and special events.*

Hop aboard a trolley for a great get-acquainted look at the city. The bright orange and green cars run on tires, not tracks. There is plenty of window space for a good view, and the clang-clang of the trolley bell adds to the fun. The trolley runs every 30 minutes.

Trolley conductors keep up a steady spiel on points of interest. They share many interesting stories about the area and are always glad to answer questions. The route covers much of the city, and it crosses the bridge to Coronado. It's exciting to look down on the bay and see the ships in the navy docks. Best of all, you can get off at any of the twelve stops and reboard whenever you like. Your ticket covers one complete loop, and it's good all day.

Old Town is a popular stop. This is where San Diego began. It's quite hilly, so wear your walking shoes. A park ranger leads a tour every weekday at 2:00 p.m., and **Old Town Tours** has daily narrated walks every hour on the hour. If you prefer to do your own thing, pick up a map at the Visitor's Center and take off. There are more than twenty restored historical buildings in the village.

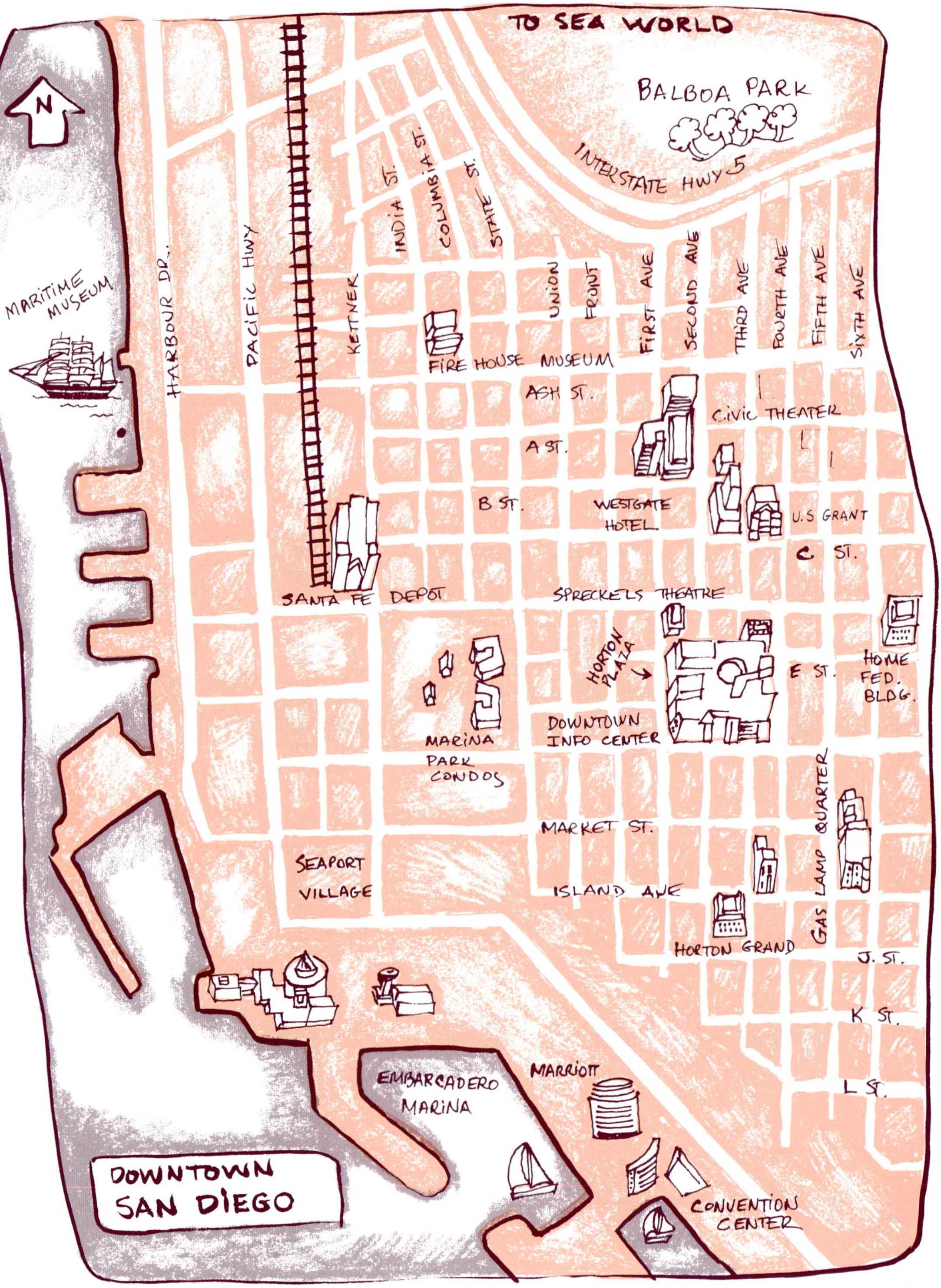
TO SEA WORLD
BALBOA PARK
INTERSTATE HWY 5
N
MARITIME MUSEUM
HARBOUR DR.
PACIFIC HWY
KETTNER
INDIA ST.
COLUMBIA ST.
STATE ST.
UNION
FRONT
FIRST AVE
SECOND AVE
THIRD AVE
FOURTH AVE
FIFTH AVE
SIXTH AVE
FIRE HOUSE MUSEUM
ASH ST.
A ST.
B ST.
CIVIC THEATER
WESTGATE HOTEL
U.S GRANT
C ST.
SANTA FE DEPOT
SPRECKELS THEATRE
HORTON PLAZA
E ST.
HOME FED. BLDG.
DOWNTOWN INFO CENTER
MARINA PARK CONDOS
MARKET ST.
GAS LAMP QUARTER
SEAPORT VILLAGE
ISLAND AVE
HORTON GRAND
J. ST.
K ST.
L ST.
MARRIOTT
EMBARCADERO MARINA
CONVENTION CENTER
DOWNTOWN SAN DIEGO

One of the oldest two-story brick buildings in California, the **Whaley House**, built in 1856, once served as a county courtroom. Restored to its original appearance, it is now a museum. Do watch for ghosts—the place is haunted.

Also in Old Town, **Seeley Stables** offers a look at transportation of the Old West, assayer's equipment, and Indian artifacts. You can visit the one-room **Mason Street School** and the **Casa de Altamirano** where the *San Diego Union* newspaper was first published.

Getting hungry? Follow your nose to the **Bazaar del Mundo**; there is food aplenty. You can choose from spicy Mexican dishes served in a patio setting or try an old favorite at the **¡Hamburguesa! La Panadera** is a bakery featuring sweet breads, coffee, and Mexican chocolate. They are famous for their churros (deep-fried pastry).

Stroll through the Bazaar's flower-filled gardens and browse the many shops. Hispanic dancers and mariachi bands frequently entertain visitors. Why not say "Hello" to the cage of colorful toucans or pose for a picture beside the prancing topiary horse hitched to an antique buggy?

Squibob Square, located next to the Visitor's Center, features specialty shops with a western theme. Wall plaques of *el sol* (the sun) smile down. There are super big chili bowls and mugs galore in the pottery shop.

Onward and upward! The hills are a bit steep, but it's worth the climb to the green lawns and Victorian buildings of **Heritage Park**. These lovely "wedding-cake" houses were moved in from their original locations and restored to their former grandeur. Some are shops and businesses; others are private homes.

San Diego kids got a chance to paint on walls. They helped artists paint the colorful murals on the pillars at the entrance ramp of the **San Diego-Coronado Bay Bridge**.

The **Derby Pendelton House** *was prefabricated in Portland, Maine, and came around Cape Horn by sailing ship in 1851. Wooden pegs were used instead of nails to put the house together.*

*Tiles in the **Serra Museum** doorway are handmade originals taken from a water-carrying flume (ditch) the padres built to irrigate their crops.*

An exquisite Victorian dollhouse is framed by the large, leaded-glass window of **Ye Olde Doll Shoppe**. The shop has dolls of every description and an unusual collection of antique trains. There are also cards and paper decorations reminiscent of the late 1800s.

It's hard to say good-bye to Old Town, but there is so much more to see and do. Get back on the trolley for a short ride to Presidio Park and **Junípero Serra Museum**. The Serra Museum is one of the most photographed buildings in San Diego. The mission-style architecture has walls three feet thick. A climb up the 81-foot tower will be rewarded with a fantastic view of Mission Bay and the city.

There are other super places to visit that are not on the trolley route. If you've ever wanted to be a fire fighter, don't miss the **Firehouse Museum** on the corner of Columbia and Cedar streets (no admission charge). Old Station 6 has been restored by the Pioneer Hook & Ladder Company. Shiny red antique trucks and engines look as if they are ready to roll on a moment's notice. Ancient leather buckets remind us there was a time when the only means of fighting a fire was the bucket brigade. You can see all kinds of protective gear for the fire fighters—from the earliest right up to the modern Darth Vader helmets.

If you're into models, the McCurdy collection of 33 miniature fire fighting apparatus is on display. And there's a large collection of fire department shoulder patches. See if you can find your city's patch.

Three horses were needed to pull the 1903 Metropolitan Steamer. Fire horses had to be intelligent, strong, and gentle. Only the best were selected for this work.

New England-bred schoolmarm Mary Walker was not impressed with San Diego. In 1865, she wrote, "It is a desolate-looking landscape. The fleas are plentiful and hungry. At recess girls smoke cigaritas and the boys amuse themselves by lassoing pigs, hens, etc."

The **Prince and the Pauper**, located at 3201 Adams Avenue, is a really different bookstore. They have hundreds of collectible and unusual children's books. Want to see what your parents or grandparents read when they were kids? Is there a special book you loved as a young child, or one you've always wanted to read? You'll probably find it here. It's hard to name a children's book the friendly clerks do not know. While you're there, be sure to meet Prince, the parrot, and McDugal, the cockatiel. They love to chat with visitors.

The **Farmer's Bazaar**, at K Street and 7th Avenue, is a good place to see, smell, and taste the culture and foods of the city. When you walk into the converted warehouse, you'll see tons of produce. There may be a 20-foot tower of red delicious apples or some exotic Asian pears. And it's hard to believe how many kinds and colors of peppers there are.

Have you ever eaten a cactus? Now's your chance. *Nopalitos* are young spineless cactus pads that are served baked, boiled, or fried. There may be baskets of red cactus fruit, too. A sweet jelly is made from its juice.

Smell the herbs and spices: vanilla beans that grow on orchid plants and bark from the cinnamon tree, garlic and bunches of cilantro, ginseng, and fresh ginger roots. Blends of the strange and the familiar fill the air.

Ethnic food booths serve specialties. Here's your chance to munch on a taco, a slice of pizza, or an egg roll, then walk through the flower market. There are orchids, ginger blossoms, and red elephant-ear anthuriums—in fact, unusual and beautiful flowers from everywhere.

A visit to California is not complete without seeing at least one of the missions. California mission-style architecture, seen throughout the state, originated with these buildings. **San Diego de Alcala,** 10818 San Diego Mission Road, was the first of the twenty-one California missions. The five-bell campanile still calls people to worship just as it did over 200 years ago. Visitors are welcome to walk through parts of the building and the gardens.

There is a small museum and the remains of adobe walls that were homes of the Mission Indians. As you look around, think of a time when fields of grain, vineyards, and livestock were cared for on the 50,000 acres of land once belonging to this mission.

A cactus sandwich is made using nopalitos *instead of bread. Boil cactus until tender. Put a slice of cheese between two pads, dip in an egg and flour batter, and grill it. You'll need a fork to eat this sandwich.*

4. Getting in the Swim

San Diego County, extending from Oceanside to the Mexican border, has seventy miles of beaches. And besides that, it has acres and acres of protected waters that are closed off from the open sea in Mission Bay and San Diego Bay. Each beach has its own character, so find one that fits your mood, grab your suit, and get in the swim.

When the Beach Boys sing "Surfin' USA," do you wish you were there? Put on your baggies and let's go! The surfing is great at **Ocean Beach**, off Interstate 8 and Sunset Cliffs Boulevard near the pier. Even if you're not a surfer, it's exciting to watch the experts ride a curl. Volleyball is big at Ocean Beach, too. Rent a ball and join the fun.

Beware: swimming in the ocean is totally different from a dip in a pool or a lake. Waves can sneak up on you, pull the sand out from under your feet, and roll you over and over in the surf. Unless you're a really good swimmer, don't go out over knee-deep. And always swim with a partner.

Lifeguard stations are located all along swimming beaches. If you're not familiar with the area, check in with the lifeguards first. They can tell you where the safest and best swimming is.

Carry plenty of sunscreen. You can get a double whammy from reflected sun rays in or near the water.

THE BEACHES

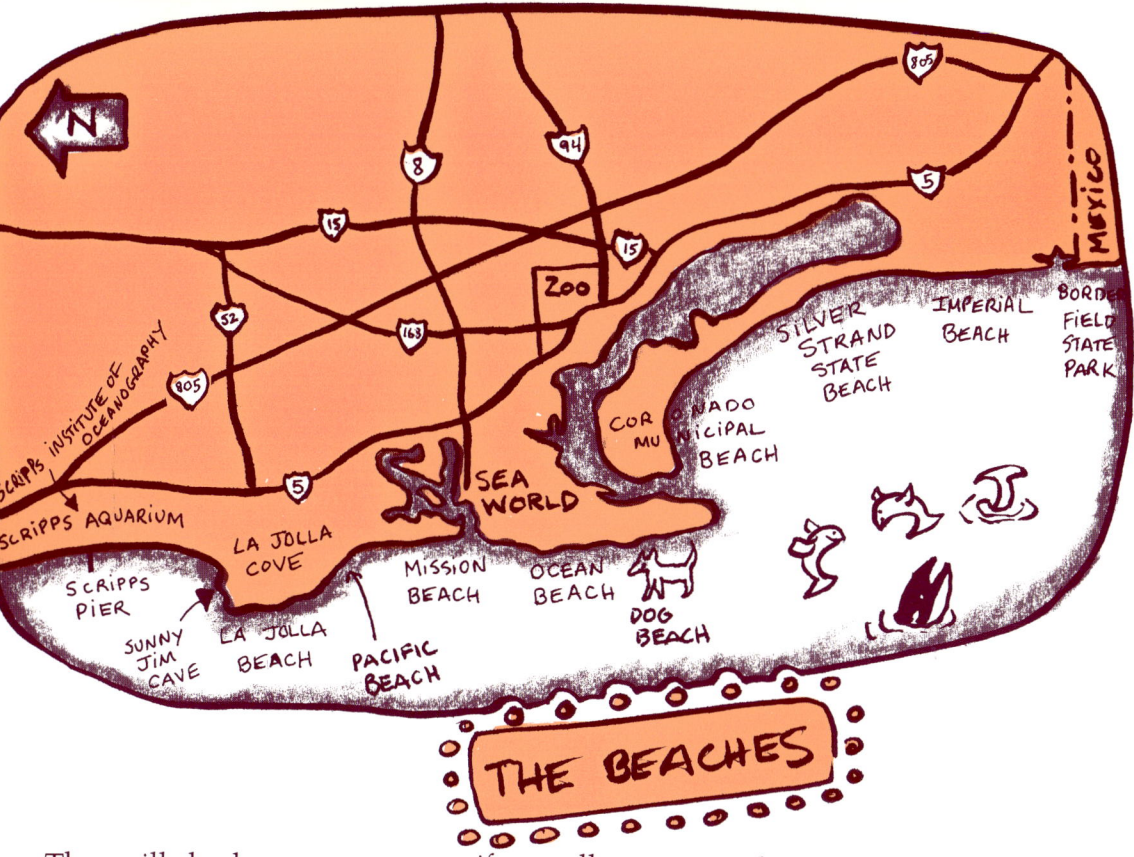

They will also keep an eye on you if you tell them you're new to ocean swimming.

La Jolla Shores Beach is super for swimmers and sunbathers. There are caves to explore, too, but be prepared for some huffing and puffing. The **Sunny Jim Cave** has 133 steps down to ocean level. Inside, you'll find fossilized shells and colorful mineral deposits in the cave walls. You can also see a collection of shells from around the world as well as other treasures from the sea.

If you've never tried tide pooling, wade in. Even the experienced "rock hopper" will enjoy La Jolla Cove's many fascinating sea creatures. Starfish, bright colored sea anemones, minnows, and hermit crabs live in the shallow pools. (Living

*Take your pooch for a run on **Dog Beach**. Four-legged visitors can enjoy the shore near Ocean Beach. Dogs are also welcome on Fiesta Island in Mission Bay. All other beaches are off-limits to canines.*

Dr. Seuss writes his whimsical children's stories in a tower overlooking La Jolla and the sea.

Tides and water and air temperatures as well as information on dangerous rip tides that can pull a swimmer out to sea are posted at lifeguard stations. Lifeguards scan the beaches continually. If you swim into trouble, raise your arms and wave. They will come to your rescue.

The Scripps research ship, **Flip***, is 355 feet long and can be flooded to stand on end. Scientists can measure temperatures, pressures, and currents from the floating laboratory. They can also study marine biology below the surface.*

ature

Torrey Pines *is named for its twisted wind-sculptured trees, the only stand of these trees on the U.S. mainland. Stand where the trees grow, and you will soon understand the power of the wind.*

sea gardens should be treated kindly. Removing or stepping on the animals can be as damaging as pulling up or stepping on plants in a flower garden.) Low tide is the time to go. Check the newspaper for tide reports.

La Jolla Cove is the place to go to snorkel or scuba dive. Beautiful fish, sea animals, and plants can be seen just a few yards off the beach. Plan to picnic on the grass, or go to nearby Scripps Park where little thatched beach huts hug the shore and offer shade.

While you're in the La Jolla area, don't miss the chance to visit the **Scripps Institute of Oceanography**, a branch of the University of California and a center for marine science research. The Scripps aquarium is open to the public, and there's a wave channel exhibit showing how waves form. You can see live creatures in a man-made tide pool, too. The very best time to go is on Wednesday and Sunday at 1:30 p.m. when the fish are fed. They really snap into action for the free lunch. Be sure to look over the large collection of books on oceanography before heading for your next stop.

Drive north up the coast for an awesome view of the Pacific. **Torrey Pines State Reserve** has some great cliff trails that overlook the ocean. If you look back to the south, you may see hanggliders sailing out on the uplifting air currents. The **Torrey Pines Glider Port** is nearby if you would like to watch them take off and land. Why not bring a picnic lunch and be a beach bum for the day.

On Mission Boulevard there's a totally different scene. This is where Pacific Beach and North and South Mission Beach are located. The boardwalk is not board; it's a wide, smooth cement walk that stretches for miles along the shore. Bikers, joggers, and skaters keep the walk alive with action. Rent a pair of roller blades and join the crowd. Kids glide skillfully along the way or roll into one of the many sidewalk cafés for a guacamole burger or a cold drink.

For a real thrill, ride the Giant Dipper roller coaster at **Belmont Park**. The Arcade at this fully restored 1925 amusement park has all the usual games and many new ones, too. The "bong" and "clang" of the videos is music to players' ears. Window-shopping in the plaza is fun. The candy-pink buildings are landscaped with flowering vines and gardens. Hungry? Then why not have lunch at one of the shoreside eateries? The **Red Onion** has terrific Mexican food.

If you prefer fresh water, take a dip in the largest indoor swimming pool west of the Mississippi. The Mission Beach **Plunge** has everything from lap swimming to scuba lessons. Or how about going to a Dive-In movie at the

Pop-eyed mudskippers are tree-climbing fish that spend most of their time on shore. They do breathe water and carry a supply in pouches above their gills—a sort of fish scuba equipment.

Plunge? You can rent your own floating seat (safety approved).

Amateurs as well as professional artists and architects play in the sand at **Imperial Beach** near the Mexican border. The sand is perfect for sculpturing, and the U.S. Open Sandcastle Competition is held here annually in July or August. There is nearly always someone at work on a masterpiece any time of year, or build your own.

Border Field State Park is for horses. If you would like to gallop along a sandy beach, this is the place to go. Horses are available, and the beach is open Thursday through Sunday from 9:00 a.m. to sunset.

There's still more. The **Coronado Municipal Beach** is across the bay from San Diego. Look for shells washed up on the white sand or just enjoy watching the waves roll in. Fires are permitted in designated areas, and it's a great place for a beach barbecue. There are campgrounds at nearby **Silver Strand State Beach**, where the calm, shallow water is ideal for families.

5. Mission Bay Park and Sea World

Both landlubbers and water bugs will find plenty to do in the 4,600-acre **Mission Bay Park** aquatic playground, also the home of Sea World. It is about half land and half water.

Mission Bay is made to order for boating. Almost every kind of floating fun is available. If you are experienced in a favorite water sport, pick up a set of park rules and head for the closest marina. For the inexperienced or those who would like a refresher course, qualified instructors are there to teach everything from sailing to waterskiing and windsurfing.

You can rent a boogie board for bodysurfing or an Aqua-Cycle Paddle Boat for an easy-does-it ride. Canoes, rowboats, speed boats, and fishing gear are also available. If all this activity boggles your mind, just relax on the sand and soak up the sun.

When your sea legs tell you it's time, switch to dry land fun. Acres of green open lawn and a steady breeze are ideal for kite flying. Watch the experts maneuver several kites at a time in a fabulous aerial ballet. Ribbon kites, box kites, bird kites—kites of every description are tugging at strings or being launched.

Mission Bay Park has 27 miles of beaches with nine areas just for swimming. Basic windsurfing is taught using a beach-land simulator, which makes learning a breeze. There are intermediate and advanced sailboards as well as kids' rigs for rent.

Campers will find a campground right at the water's edge. **Campland on the Bay** *is open year-round. Make reservations early, though. It's always full of fun-seeking visitors.*

San Diego is home to world champion diver Greg Louganis. Greg won gold medals for both platform and springboard in the 1984 Olympics and repeated his sweep of the Olympic diving events in 1988.

If tennis is your game, you won't find better year-round weather for it. There are more than 1,200 private and public courts in San Diego County.

Miles of biking and jogging paths follow the coast or wind through landscaped gardens. This is a great way to see more of the park. Volleyball nets and soccer fields invite friendly games. And balls, bikes, and all sorts of sports equipment can be rented.

For a real California-style picnic, plan a beach barbecue. Fire pits and tables are located all along the bay. Grassy areas are best (sand has a way of getting into picnic baskets). Watch the sun go down on a perfect day, or visit **Hospitality Point** for a pop concert under the stars. The San Diego Symphony often features well-known stage acts in its Mission Bay performances. Bring a blanket to sit on while you enjoy the music.

Check out the tower with the flag flying from its top. It's right in the center of **Sea World** and can be seen from all over Mission Bay. Nearly everyone has heard of Shamu the killer whale. Here he is with Baby Shamu and friends to dazzle you in a super aquatic show. Don't sit in the first six rows of the stadium, though, unless you don't mind getting wet. Shamu loves to splash visitors.

Plan to spend a full day in Sea World. There's so much to see and do you won't want to miss a thing. Start off the morning at the **Penguin Encounter** where the guides, not the birds, are trained. They enter the penguins' frosty home to serve them a fishy breakfast and to identify the many different species for visitors.

A moving walk takes you by the enclosure.

Sea World has special facilities for disabled guests including TDD (telecommunication device for the deaf). There are also rows of cute dolphin-shaped strollers for use by families with small tots.

23

It's subfreezing weather for the polar penguins. Ten thousand pounds of fresh snow is blown in daily to keep them happy. The enclosure is designed to look as much like Antarctica as possible. But leave your parka at home. It's people comfort on your side of the glass.

Everyone gets an up-front look. Of course, you can ride as many times as you like or stand on an upper level to watch these black and white comics as long as you wish.

If you've never come face to face with a moray eel, now is your chance. Underpool viewing at **Forbidden Reef** gives you a close-up look as they slither through the rocks. Moray eels are completely harmless unless threatened, even though they have a bad case of ugly. At the surface of the pool, bat rays stick up their noses puppylike to be fed or petted.

Veteran sea lion actors Clyde and Seamore had better watch out. They're forever being upstaged by an otter who plays the part of a bilge rat in the hilarious production, **"Pirates of Pinniped."** The otter doesn't always come in on cue, which adds to the laughs.

Find your way to **Places of Learning.** There is a circle of state flags and a one-acre map of the United States. It's fun to look for your home state and its capital, but be careful not to step in the Gulf of Mexico—it's wet.

For chills and thrills, visit the 400,000-gallon **Shark Exhibit.** But never fear, the acrylic plastic viewing panel could support the weight of 40 bull elephants—over 240 tons. While you're there, be sure to take a look at a model of the jaw of an ancestor of the great white shark. Its dental bill wouldn't have amounted to much: when one tooth broke off or wore down, a new one just moved up to take its place. Sharks still have multiple rows of teeth.

For a change of pace, find a seat in "City Streets" to see a 1930 version of Colonel Sullivan's Radio Show. You'll probably want to sing along with the kids in the old-time song and dance routines.

25

6. Yachts and Yachts of Ships and Boats

It's handy to learn a few nautical terms so you won't be lost at sea. The front of a ship is the bow; *the rear is the* stern. *To go* aft *is to go the the rear. Starboard is the right side of a ship when you face forward, and* port *is on your left. Now you won't be mistaken for a landlubber.*

Oh, for the life of a sailor. A narrated tour of the harbor is a good place to begin. The 2-hour, 25-mile excursion offers a look at one of the world's best natural harbors. Board your craft at the foot of Broadway on Harbor Drive and be prepared for an exciting cruise. During peak tourist season, you might want to buy your tickets early in the day to be sure you get a seat.

The boats make a double loop around Coronado Island, under the bridge and past navy ships. You may see one of the huge aircraft carriers, or several destroyers, or perhaps a sub will be in port at the nuclear submarine pier.

Your guide may point out merchant vessels from all over the world, sleek yachts out for a sail, and the U.S. Coast Guard Station. As you pass Point Loma, you'll see where Cabrillo and his men first sailed into the harbor nearly 500 years ago.

Three vintage vessels make up the floating **Maritime Museum** located at the foot of A Street. The *Star of India* is a square-rigged windjammer. Visitors walk up a squeaky gangplank to board the iron-hulled tall ship. A seagull is usually circling her rigging, and it's easy to imagine the captain shouting "Hoist anchor" and the wind filling her sails. She does still sail in the bay on special occasions.

Next to the *Star of India*, the turn-of-the-century *Berkeley* rides at ease. She served as a passenger ferry for sixty years crossing the bay between San Francisco and Oakland. The *Berkeley* carried refugees to safety after the earthquake and fire of 1906. She has been restored but does not get under way. There are a number of maritime exhibits to see on board the ferry, such as a history of ferryboats, photographs, and ship models.

The third part of the floating museum is the steam yacht, *Medea*. Built in 1904, she was a luxury boat of the time. Visitors can go aboard to peek into the elegant cabins; caretakers see that she is kept in mint condition. The *Medea* served in both world wars, and the grand old lady still steams out into the bay from time to time.

If all this seafaring has given you an appetite, **Anthony's Fish Grotto** is right next door. The fish-and-chips is super, and if you can get a window table, it's fun to watch the pelicans checking out the fishing boats for a handout.

Would you like to go aboard a **navy ship**? Every Saturday and Sunday between 1:00 p.m. and 4:00 p.m. the navy holds open house on one or more of the ships docked on Broadway Pier. Navy personnel will show you through the ship from stem to stern. The visit is free—courtesy of your tax dollars.

When you need shore leave, pay a visit to **Seaport Village** on Harbor Drive. This is a bayside cluster of shops and restaurants, with a park next door. There's *always* something going on:

The garibaldi is California's state marine fish. It looks like a large goldfish with silver-blue eyes. Garibaldis often gather to stare back at the passengers on board Santa Catalina's glass-bottomed boats.

Guacamole is a dip or spread made from cool green avocados with a zap of hot chili salsa. It's a taste sensation.

27

The Star of India, *launched in 1863, is the world's oldest merchant ship still afloat. She made 21 around-the-world voyages carrying immigrants from England to New Zealand and cargo to India. From 1901 to 1923, she sailed the icy waters of Alaska for the salmon fishing industry. The* Star *certainly earned her California retirement.*

the Seaport Village Brass Band may be giving a concert in the gazebo; Kazoo, the mime, may be wandering through the streets giving impromptu performances; jugglers and magicians are everywhere; and you don't have to wait for the 4th of July to see fireworks.

Bring a picnic lunch or buy take-out food from one of the many eateries. The park is a great place to relax and watch the boats sail in the bay. Kite flying is a favorite sport here, and there's a shop that sells just kites, all sorts of kites from all over the world.

Beware of the seagulls! They can spot a picnic from across the bay. Although they *are* fun to feed, they can get quite pesky and are known to snatch food right out of a hand—sometimes nipping a finger in the act.

Have you seen the little ferryboats chugging back and forth across the bay? They're a San Diego tradition. When the Coronado bridge was completed, the ferry service was discontinued. But people missed the little boats, so now they're running again. It's a fun way to get over to Coronado. The boats are for pedestrians only, though bicycles are permitted. The ferry runs every hour on the hour.

Some of the world's best sportfishing is in San Diego's offshore waters. Charter boat companies from Oceanside all the way to Mexico offer fishing adventures for beginners and experts. Check out the landings in Point Loma off Rosecrans Street. If you're there when the boats come in, you can see what's being caught.

A half-day trip to the offshore kelp beds is sure to keep you busy pulling in a good catch. You might even hook the "big one." A full day trip to the Coronado Islands in Mexico is a fisherman's dream. Many boats carry fish finders, and an experienced crew knows where the hot spots are. Tackle rental is available.

If you would like to try your luck from one of the fishing piers, go ahead! Good catches are made from all five San Diego County piers. Bait houses rent tackle and can tell you what is being caught that day and what bait to use.

Many people come to San Diego just to see the whales. From December through mid-February, gray whales migrate along the coast on their way to the warm calving waters of Baja California in Mexico. It's possible to see the whales from shore, but for a closer look, you can book a **whale watching** excursion. Check the newspaper or "Arts, Activities and Attractions" for lists of

Whalers nearly exterminated the gray whale before laws were passed to protect them. Now twelve to thirteen thousand of these giants pass the San Diego coast each year during the winter migration.

Fishing boats bob around a lot. If motion sickness is a problem for you, use medication that has been prescribed by a doctor—before you leave the dock.

What to do with all the fish? Have your catch canned or frozen and shipped home. Packing companies are available near the landings.

companies offering these trips. Watch for water spouts when you're out there; the whales usually travel in herds.

There are some one-day cruises available: **Catalina Island Seajet** cruise leaves from San Diego B Street Terminal or Oceanside Harbor at the Lighthouse. Both the M/V *Maria G* and the M/V *Renna G* are computer stabilized for a smooth ride. This is a real sea cruise, and you have about five hours to explore the island before the return trip. On Catalina, you can arrange a tour of Avalon or a trip on a glass-bottom boat for a look at undersea life.

The **Ensenada Express** sails at 9:00 a.m. from the B Street Pier for a full day of adventure. You'll get a close-up look at Mexico's Coronado Islands and have about five hours to explore and shop in the Mexican city of Ensenada. This is not a trip kids should do on their own. Take along a parent or other adult.

If you happen to be visiting during December, there are several awesome displays of Christmas lights to see. Decorated and brightly lit boats go on parade, at different harbors, throughout the month. Check "What's Doing" or "Go" in the local newspaper for information.

To see experts maneuver their boats any time of year, visit the **San Diego Princess Model Yacht Basin** on Vacation Isle in Mission Bay. Every weekend, modelers sail their crafty little remote-controlled boats, and they hold some very exciting races. Come to cheer for your favorite. The show is free.

7. Past, Present, and Future

In the middle of Balboa Park, there is a wide walkway called *El Prado*, and there are sixteen museums right here. With so much to see, it's hard to know where to start.

One possibility is the **Reuben H. Fleet Space Theater and Science Center**, which has more than fifty hands-on exhibits. They've dreamed up some really neat ways to explore the principles of science. For instance, try stirring things up in a resonant bowl. You'll find a large Oriental-looking metal dish full of water. Run your fingers around and around the top edge of the bowl: the water will begin to vibrate, fizz, foam, and bubble all of its own accord. You can get an inside look at how the heart works in another exhibit, or make water run up hill with an "Archimedes screw." It's so much fun you won't realize how much you're learning.

You can travel to other planets, to the ocean depths, or inside the human body in **Space Theater** films. They may be showing an erupting volcano or exotic cultures of other lands. The program changes every few weeks. There are evening programs, too. You can even see a laser-light concert choreographed to popular music.

"A Passport to Balboa Park," available at the House of Hospitality, may save you some money, depending on the amount of time you have and what you would like to see.

*There is plenty of free parking in **Balboa Park**, but do not leave anything of value in your car, not even in the trunk. Thieves are expert at springing locks, and car break-ins are common.*

Want to see a 2,800-pound gemstone? "Big Thumper" is a jade boulder that was found in 8 feet of water offshore at Big Sur, California.

Street performers do their thing on the **Prado**. Mimes, magicians, unicyclists, and musicians entertain for a pass-the-hat donation. You might even find yourself part of an act as these talented people amuse or confuse the audience.

Would you like a close look at desert life? The **Natural History Museum**'s computer touch screen lets kids see, hear, and touch to learn about desert ecology. Another hands-on exhibit is in the endangered species hall. First stroke a tiger skin (it was confiscated from illegal hunters), then learn more about threatened and extinct animals.

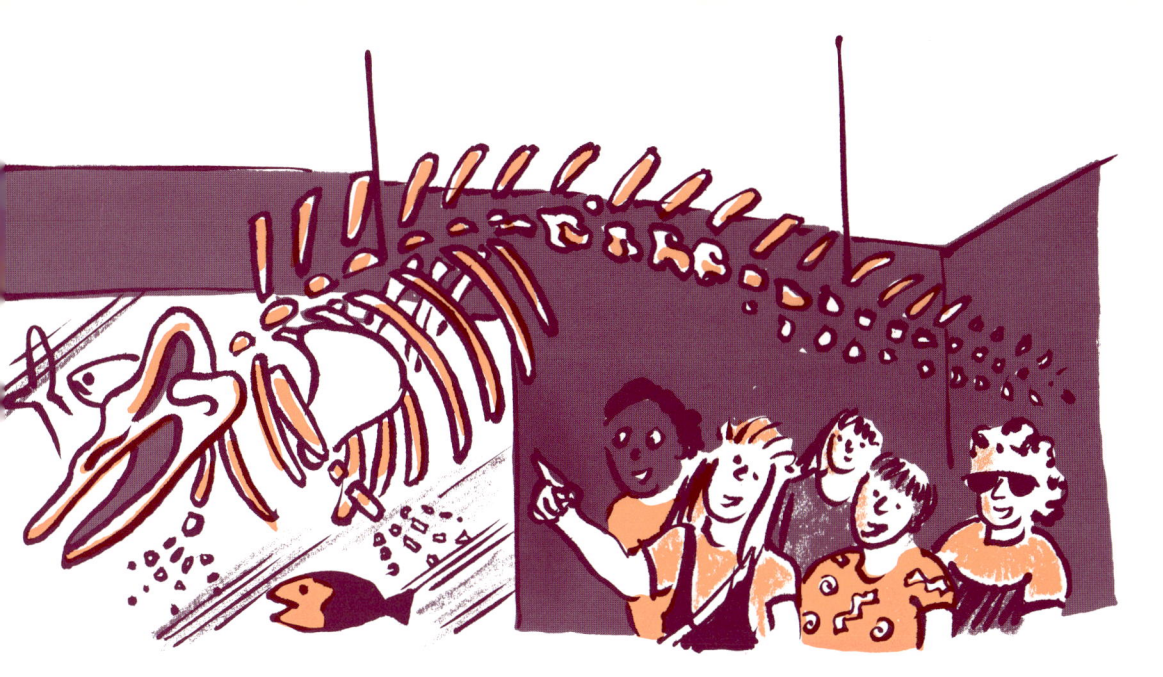

A curved skeleton of a goose-beaked whale hangs over the sea display. And a stuffed specimen of the strange oarfish could easily be mistaken for a sea monster. Rock hounds and pebble puppies will enjoy the gems and minerals display in the Mineral Gallery. There are multicolored tourmalines, blue topaz, and orange garnets, all from San Diego County mines.

On down the Prado, there's a reflecting pool where waterlilies and lotus bloom year-round. Just behind it is a Victorian greenhouse in the **Botanical Gardens**. Orchids and other tropical plants grow here in a jungle environment.

Cross the walkway to the **Hall of Champions** where San Diego honors outstanding athletes representing over forty sports. There are photographs, mementos, trophies, and histories of the champions. You can ask a computer for Padres baseball facts or see a blue and gold Charger football jersey or try your skill on a video golf putting-green.

A movie theater features continuous sports films at the Hall of Champions. Laugh or groan at the bloopers while you rest your feet.

*San Diego's **U.S. Olympic Training Center** is scheduled for completion in 1993. Visitors will get to see some of our top athletes train for the gold.*

*The **San Diego Sockers** have won eight championships in the Major Indoor Soccer League. That's something to remember for your next "Sports Trivia" game.*

On his famous walk, astronaut Harrison (Jack) Schmitt collected a moon rock for each state in the Union. California's moon rock is on display in the Aerospace Museum. Does it look any different from some of the rocks found right here on Planet Earth?

The Aerospace Museum sponsors an annual contest for young modelers of San Diego County. Winners may display their models in the museum until the next year's competition.

Would you like to see a pro ball game? The **Chargers** (NFL) play home games in Jack Murphy Stadium from August through December. The **Padres** (NL) are seldom rained out when they play on their home diamond, also at Jack Murphy Stadium (the season is April through September). Do you get a kick out of soccer? From October through April, the **San Diego Sockers** (MISL) play home games in the San Diego Sports Arena. San Diego has a hockey team, too. It's called the **Gulls**.

Trains and scenery are reduced to scale size in the **Model Railroad Museum**, and there's a real operating semaphore (moving arm signals). There's enough stuff here to dazzle any railroad buff. The museum is open Friday, Saturday, and Sunday.

The **Museum of Man** traces the cultural history of man through the ages, especially that of the Americas. Demonstrations of weaving and tortilla making are held each week, Wednesday through Sunday.

Just south of the Prado is the **Aerospace Museum**. You can't miss it—there's a navy jet parked in the front yard. A journey through the history of flight begins in the International Aerospace Hall of Fame, where you can check out portraits and memorabilia of aviation greats.

A replica of the Red Baron's Fokker Dr. 1 is displayed in the World War I exhibit. It's the bright red plane with the black German crosses, and it has three wings. It could outclimb and outrun almost any Allied aircraft of the time.

Life-size barnstormers and their aircraft demonstrate "The Golden Age of Flight," 1919 to 1939. Almost everyone recognizes Lindbergh's plane, "The Spirit of St. Louis." The full-sized replica was assembled by museum volunteers, including three of the men who helped build the original plane right here in San Diego.

Original fighters from World War II have been carefully restored. You can see a Spitfire, Stuka, Zero, and Navy Hellcat; all are ready to fly. A Curtiss P-40 Flying Tiger displays its famous toothy grin. There is an F-86 and a MiG-15 in the Jet Age area, which also has other jet aircraft, jet engines, and various artifacts.

Beam up to the Space Age. Replicas of the Mercury, Gemini, and Apollo are here, along with photos of Neil Armstrong taking man's first step on the moon. A cross-section model of the Space Shuttle gives an idea of the cramped space astronauts live and work in. Try a taste of astronaut ice cream. Freeze-dried neapolitan is tasty (if you don't have the real thing).

*The Space Theater's **OMNIMAX** is the cinema of the future. Pictures are ten times the size of those in regular theaters. They are projected on a giant tilted dome screen to make it seem like you are really there and a part of the action.*

Women in Aviation are honored in a special exhibit. Mannequins model WASP uniforms. Jacqueline Cockran helped to organize and then led the Woman's Air Force Service Pilots of World War II. Pictures and histories of astronaut Sally Ride and cosmonaut Valentina Fereshkova are there beside those of Harriet Quimby, who in 1911 was the first woman in America to become a licensed pilot.

If you haven't found your favorite aircraft, look over the model collection. There are more than 800 displayed in cases and hanging from the ceiling.

Still raring to go? There are three art museums located on the Prado. The **San Diego Museum of Art** exhibits fine art through the ages. Traveling collections and special exhibits such as "Young Art," art by San Diego students of all grade levels, are shown.

The Timken Art Gallery offers a collection of famous American and European paintings. And it also has an outdoor sculpture garden—a good

Katherine Wright assisted her brothers, Orville and Wilbur in the construction of their first aircraft. Too bad she hasn't received more credit for her efforts.

place to give your feet a rest. Admission to the Timken is free.

Most people like to take pictures. Some of the very best taken by both professionals and amateurs may be seen in the **Museum of Photographic Arts**. It includes still photography, video, and motion picture works. The museum programs have changing exhibits as well as film and video shows.

The large round building with all the colorful murals just south of the Prado is the **Centro Cultural de la Raza**. Inside there is an ongoing display of Indian, Mexican, and Chicano (Americans of Mexican descent) arts and crafts.

Have you ever seen a living museum? Cannons roar and swords flash at the annual December reenactment of the battle of San Pasqual at the **San Pasqual Battlefield State Historic Park** in Escondido. Festivities include an 1846 Charro and U.S. Dragoons encampment, folk dancing, and a barbecue dinner.

Need help getting that special snapshot? You can get pointers on how to take better pictures at the Museum of Photographic Arts.

8. Who's for the Zoo?

There are more than 3,500 animals to see in the **San Diego Zoo**. Flamingo Lagoon is just inside the entrance. The bright pink birds among the tropical plants make great color pictures. If it's nesting season, you may want to hold your nose. The strange odor is a natural occurrence; the birds are on a special diet during this time. Flamingos build mud towers for nests—a good idea, because with legs like theirs, it's a long way to the ground.

Double-decker buses travel the zoo roads to give passengers a look at residents. The drivers know many strange facts and funny stories about the animals. Bears wait for the buses and playfully beg for goodies.

Take the **Skyfari** for a bird's-eye view of the zoo and a look at the ocean and the countryside. The tram travels up to 170 feet above the ground.

Either the bus or the Skyfari will give you a good idea of where the different exhibits are located and which ones you want to visit again. But the very best way to see the zoo is on foot. Get a map from the ticket office and take off.

Follow a dry riverbed through a jungle of palm, fig, and coral trees. This is tiger country! Zoo

In the 1920s, Balboa Park was infested with rattlesnakes. The San Diego Zoo paid part of its expenses by trapping, selling, and trading local rattlers.

workers have created a three-acre rain forest home for 35 animal species that are native to this environment.

Crocodiles bask in the sun or go for a swim. Bright tropical birds call out or peer from the reeds in their man-made marsh. A mud wallow gives creature comforts to a pair of tapirs. Stop to admire or shiver at the Burmese python.

Then it's on to see the tigers. They may be splashing in their pools (tigers enjoy swimming). Notice how much they resemble house cats when they groom their golden fur or stretch out for a snooze.

Scripps Aviary is a close encounter with the bird world. A huge landscaped flight cage is complete with a waterfall and fully grown trees. Walk right in. A chorus of cheeps, chirps, and whistles will greet you. Look up, down, and all around. Birds are everywhere.

A red circle with a white E in the center is the symbol for endangered animal species. Take a good look at any animal with this mark by its name. You could be the last generation to see this species alive.

Keepers wear face shields when they feed venom-spitting cobras. The snake takes deadly aim for its victim's eyes and seldom misses.

Goolara is one of only two albino (white) koalas known to exist in the world. His name is an Australian aboriginal word meaning "moonlight."

The Galápagos tortoise is believed to be the longest-lived animal on earth. Some are thought to be at least 150 years old, and they can weigh more than 500 pounds. Early sailing ships stopped at the Galápagos Islands to carry away the huge animals for a source of fresh meat.

Tiny hummingbirds from both North and South America have their own aviary. They flash jewellike colors as they dart from flower to feeder. The birds feel so much at home that many of them build nests and raise young.

The San Diego Zoo is one of the few places in the world where you can see koalas outside their native Australia. These furry little animals with their large ears and button eyes look as though they belong on a toy shelf.

When your feet need a rest, take in one of the animal shows. Animals in Action demonstrates how animals hunt for food or keep from being someone else's dinner. At the Animal Chit Chat show, you may meet Arusha, an African cheetah, and Anna, a golden retriever. Besides sharing the stage, the cat and dog are roommates and the best of friends.

Kids of all ages enjoy the Children's Zoo where they can have direct contact with the animals. Be gentle; sudden movement or loud noises may startle and upset them. You can pet a fawn or a rabbit, or watch chickens and ducks hatch in a glass-enclosed incubator. Best of all, take a peek in the nursery windows where young animals are cared for. You might see a baby wallaby looking out of an improvised pouch made of towels, or a tiny gazelle being bottle fed.

San Diego Wild Animal Park is an auxiliary of the zoo. It's located in the farmlands less than an hour's drive from Balboa Park. Herds of elephants, rhinoceroses, antelopes, and other endangered species roam the large compounds. Many young are born in the "just like home" habitats. Some animals are sold or exchanged with zoos around the world. Others are released in their native land to rebuild a vanished population.

Be prepared for an exciting new zoo experience as you enter through the Africa-styled Nairobi Village. Hop aboard the Wagasa Bush Line for a safari into Africa and Asia. The pollution-free monorail glides quietly through the park without disturbing the creatures. Visitors see the animals going about the business of eating,

Ever see a green polar bear? Blue-green algae that live in the animals' freshwater pool sometimes enter their hollow guard hairs, giving the bears a green tint. The algae don't cause any harm, but the bears do look a little strange.

sleeping, and caring for their young almost as they do in the wild.

On the plains, you might see a 150-pound newborn baby whose mom is a white rhino or Blackjack, a Ugandan giraffe, who is the dominant male of his herd. Bales of special browse are hoisted into "feeder trees" so the long-necked diners can eat at a natural level.

Meanwhile, back in Nairobi Village, animal shows are ready to begin. The Bird Show stars a free-flying cast and a kooky little parrot that roller skates. The Elephant Wash is a favorite of zoo visitors—trainers usually get a bath, too.

Make friends with a meerkat at Critter Encounter. These are the funny little animals that stand upright on top of their burrows looking for all the world like a bunch of commuters waiting for the 5:40.

At the Petting Krall, you can touch some of the hand-raised exotic species. Hornbills are real characters. They like to ride on the sheep's backs, pull the antelope's tails, and sometimes untie people's shoelaces.

Right next door is the Animal Care Center where sick or orphaned babies are looked after. Windows allow visitors to watch food preparation and the feeding of young animals. There are always a variety of newborns to be seen.

If watching the lunch bunch has given you the hungries, the Savannah Picnic Grove is a good place to eat and relax. If you didn't pack a basket, there are several restaurants in the Village. And try a Safari Cone—a rolled crisp waffle filled with ice cream and your choice of several outlandish toppings. You'll need a spoon to eat it.

Ready to hike? Do the Kilimanjaro Trail for a

How do you find a missing zebra? Stripes are zebra "fingerprints." Each animal has a different stripe pattern, even those of the same species.

closer look at some of the large animals. Or take a walk through the Australian rain forest, which may make you think of a South Pacific island. Ferns, seven varieties of eucalyptus, and other exotic plants create a homey atmosphere for rainbow lorikeets, pink cockatoos, and dozens of other tropical birds.

Many of the unusual plants in the park serve a dual purpose. They not only create different habitats but provide food as well. Exotic groceries play a big part in keeping the animals well and happy.

Along the Kilimanjaro Trail and throughout the park there are special gardens containing rare and endangered plants. Ten major life zones— from desert to mountains— are represented. Proteas, strangely beautiful flowers from Africa, bloom most of the year. And there are huge aloes, palmlike cycads, and cacti.

More money has been spent on plants than on animals in the Wild Animal Park. Many special plants are irreplaceable. Bonsai trees are so valuable they are chained down to protect them from theft. These minature trees flower, bear fruit, and go through seasonal change just like full-sized specimens. They can live for many years and become heirlooms to be passed down from generation to generation.

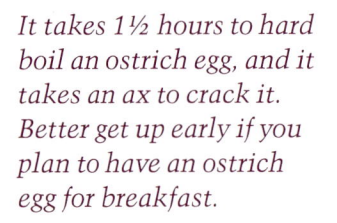

It takes 1½ hours to hard boil an ostrich egg, and it takes an ax to crack it. Better get up early if you plan to have an ostrich egg for breakfast.

At the upper loop on the trail there are three lath or shade houses. The epiphyllum garden grows in hundreds of hanging pots. These long flat-leaved plants, members of the cactus family, are rather ugly—until they bloom, when each plant may have dozens of large delicate flowers.

The fuchsia garden blooms beside a 15-foot waterfall. Next to it is a wonderland of bonsai plants. You may feel like a giant as you wander through evergreen forests no more than two feet high.

Now complete the loop back to Nairobi Village. You've experienced a carefully planned ecosystem of plants and animals.

The **San Diego Ostrich Ranch** is a working ranch, but visitors are welcome. Large fenced areas hold more than a hundred birds. There are usually babies, females, nests of eggs, and stately black-plumed males to be seen. Approach the pens quietly, and pay attention to the sign "Beware, We Bite"—they do, and hard.

Ostrich products may be seen in the gift shop. A half eggshell in a glass case has a branch inside it holding a hummingbird nest and two tiny eggs. The size comparison is amazing.

9. Grease Paint, Galleries, and Glitz

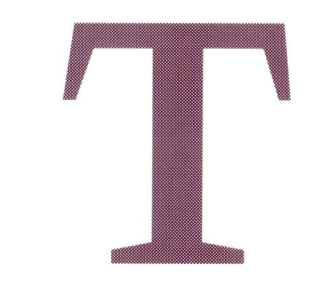

Times Arts TIX Center at Horton Plaza offers half-price day-of-performance tickets and full-price advance sale tickets for all of the performing arts.

Tickets to the **San Diego Repertory Theatre** assure you of some very special entertainment. The company presents both contemporary plays and classics in the elegant **Lyceum Theatre**. The annual production of Dickens's *Christmas Carol* is always a sell-out. They offer Saturday and Sunday matinees as well as evening performances. The Lyceum is down the curved staircase in the lower level in Horton Plaza.

If you prefer the movies, **Horton Plaza** also has a seven-screen cinema complex showing the latest films. After the show, look for the street performers. They often come out to entertain in the evenings.

Go up the wide stairs leading to the main level of the plaza. Landscaping is an art in San Diego, and the Horton has gone all out. Topiary trees and shrubs make a plant zoo. There are dancing bears, hippos, and elephants. During holidays, the animals may be wearing seasonal decorations.

Sunday in Balboa Park is special. The **House of Pacific Relations** ("Pacific" meaning peaceful, not ocean) is a group of sixteen small cottages with exhibits on the culture, history, and traditions of different countries. Each Sunday after-

45

Topiary is the art of training trees and shrubs into fanciful shapes. Animals, balls, and even castles grow with the help of skillful gardeners.

Under certain weather conditions, it's possible to hear the Spreckels Organ for a distance of more than two miles. A 20 horsepower electric blower provides the tremendous volume of air needed to operate the instrument.

noon, from March through October, there is an open house. Members wear their national costumes and serve special refreshments. You might want to try scones in "Scotland," poppyseed cakes in "Czechoslovakia," and litchi nuts in "China."

Be sure to save room for lunch with the country that is the chosen host for that week. Music and folk dancing programs are held on an outdoor stage. There is a charge or a requested donation for food, but a visit to the houses and the program is free.

Just across the boulevard from the cottages, the **Spreckels Organ Pavilion** will probably be getting ready for the regular 2:00 Sunday afternoon concert. It houses the world's largest outdoor pipe organ: some of the 4,416 individual pipes are over 32 feet tall; the smallest is less than one-half inch long. There is no charge for the concert.

During summer evenings, other musical performances are held at the pavilion. With 2,400 seats, there's plenty of room. Check with the **House of Hospitality** on the Prado for a list of what's going on.

If you're a Pinocchio or Punch and Judy fan, you'll really like the **Marie Hitchcock Theatre**. The show stars puppets, marionettes, and hand-rod characters in funny skits and plays.

The **San Diego Civic Light Opera** offers musicals in Balboa Park's outdoor **Starlight Bowl**. Just imagine "Peter Pan" or another favorite being performed under the stars.

While strolling down the Prado you may come upon some wooden buildings that make you think you've taken a wrong turn and wound up in Merrie Olde England. You've actually found the **Old Globe Theatre**, designed in typical Elizabethan-style architecture. Players in costume often come out into the courtyard to advertise the current show by dancing and singing.

Ikebana, the Japanese art of flower arranging, is demonstrated in Balboa Park each spring, and almost every weekend, the **Casa del Prado** has a flower exhibit, which may feature bonsai (dwarfed) plants, exotic orchids, or lovely camellias. Just wander through, or stay a while to enjoy the show.

In the same building, you can see young thespians perform for the preteen and teen crowd. The **Junior Theatre** has performances on Friday evening and Saturday and Sunday afternoons.

In downtown San Diego, the **Civic Theatre** offers the best in classical entertainment. It's home to the San Diego Opera as well as touring ballet and folk dance companies.

And now for something different. If you're a whodunit fan, you're in for a real treat at the **Imperial House Restaurant's Mystery Cafe**. Help solve the crime and enjoy a four-course dinner at the same time! It's very popular, so make reservations well in advance.

Fantastic prices are paid for rare orchids. Collectors brave crocodile-infested swamps, jungles, and yellow fever to find some of these flower treasures.

10. Cabrillo, Coronado, and Chula Vista

*Erosion and sudden gusts of wind are at work on the face of the cliffs at **Point Loma**. For safety's sake, stay on the trails, and keep well back from the edge of the cliffs. It's a long way down.*

Cabrillo National Monument is located within the city limits on the tip of Point Loma (that long finger of land pointing south). The visitors center will give you maps and brochures, including a schedule of programs for the day. They also have exhibits of Cabrillo's voyage that include models of his ships, the *San Salvador* and the *Victoria*. Imagine sailing into the unknown aboard one of these small, frail ships.

From the overlook, there is a fantastic view of the Pacific Ocean and the harbor. An impressive statue of Juan Rodríguez Cabrillo stands on the bluff; he holds his sword in one hand and his navigational instruments in the other. Video programs in the auditorium include an account of his historic voyage.

The **Old Point Loma lighthouse** stands as it did more than one hundred years ago when the keeper first lit the oil lamp. Climbing the winding stairs to see the huge light is like taking a trip back in time. You're bound to wonder how many ships were guided to safe harbor by its beacon.

The visitors center has a wheelchair ramp and an electric shuttle to take disabled people to and from the lighthouse. There are some cold drink machines but no food service in the park.

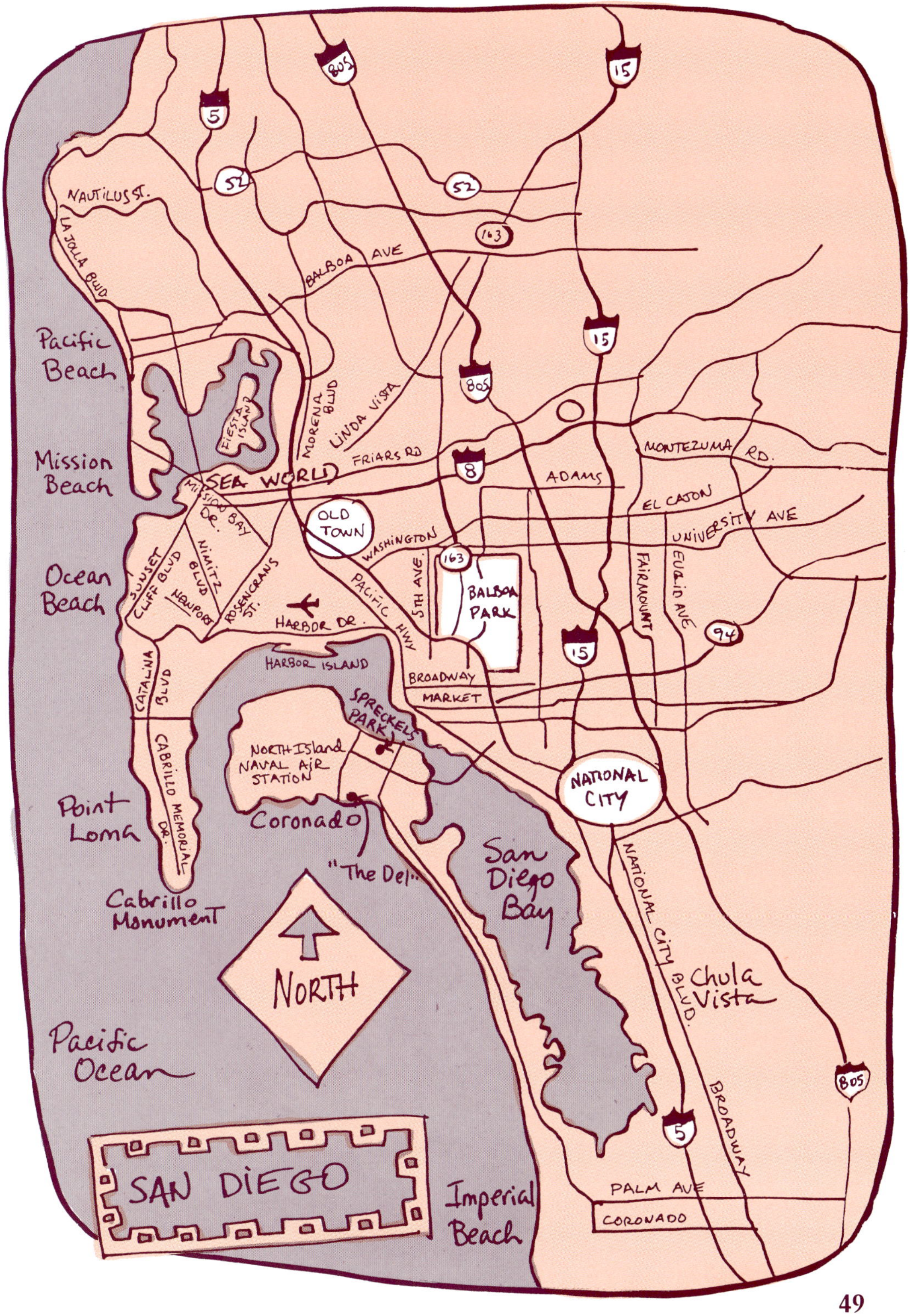
NAUTILUS ST.
LA JOLLA BLVD
BALBOA AVE
Pacific Beach
FIESTA ISLAND
MORENA BLVD
LINDA VISTA
FRIARS RD
Mission Beach
SEA WORLD
MISSION BAY DR.
MONTEZUMA RD.
ADAMS
EL CAJON
UNIVERSITY AVE
OLD TOWN
WASHINGTON
SUNSET CLIFF BLVD
NIMITZ BLVD
NEWPORT
ROSECRANS ST.
Ocean Beach
PACIFIC HWY
5TH AVE.
BALBOA PARK
FAIRMOUNT
EUCLID AVE
HARBOR DR.
HARBOR ISLAND
BROADWAY
MARKET
CATALINA BLVD
SPRECKELS PARK
North Island NAVAL AIR STATION
CABRILLO MEMORIAL DR.
Point Loma
Coronado
NATIONAL CITY
"The Del"
San Diego Bay
NATIONAL CITY BLVD.
Cabrillo Monument
NORTH
Chula Vista
Pacific Ocean
BROADWAY
SAN DIEGO
PALM AVE
CORONADO
Imperial Beach

The sea anemone is an animal that is often mistaken for a plant. When undisturbed, it opens up a fringe of tentacles that look like flower petals. It is carnivorous (flesh-eating) and can catch small fish in its waving tentacles.

Most rays are harmless creatures that feed on plankton and crustaceans. They use their flattened winglike pectoral fins to "fly" through the water. Waders beware! Stepping on a sting ray is a painful experience.

Hike the two-mile **Bayside Nature Trail** where shrubbery is kept low by constant winds from the sea. You may see many small landbirds, as the area is on the north-south flyway for migrating species. Seabirds shriek and call as they play in the uplifting air currents. You can also see remnants of a coastal artillery system placed to defend the harbor during World Wars I and II.

Some of the best tide pooling in California is on the western side of Point Loma. Explore the pools during low tide to see flowerlike anemones wave their tentacles in the still water, crabs scurrying about, pink and brown starfish clinging to the rocks, and maybe even a shy octopus.

You might be tempted to shake hands with the strange sponge called "dead man's fingers," but remember this is a delicate ecosystem that can easily be destroyed by thoughtless persons. All of the creatures are protected by law, and nothing should be taken from the tide pools. A ranger is often on duty and can help you locate interesting creatures or identify some you've found.

In winter, whales swim in close to shore as they round the point on their way to Mexico. There is a special viewing station with a glass front to cut off the sea winds. During the migration, rangers present programs on the natural history of the whales. They show some super film shots of these fabulous animals.

The viewing station is also a good place to watch the many boats and ships entering and leaving the harbor. The big navy ships are always exciting. Tankers and merchant vessels from around the world also sail in and out. There may be one from Russia, or Japan, or England. It's fun to identify them by the flags they fly.

The **U.S. Marine Corps Recruit Depot Command Museum** exhibits history of the M.C.R.D. from 1846 to the present. The museum is located on the base next to Point Loma. On Friday afternoons, you can watch a military review.

From Point Loma, you can see that **Coronado** is not actually an island. A long strip of sand called the Silver Strand connects it to the mainland. San Diegans have always called it an island, though, and the U.S. Naval Air Station, occupying over half of Coronado, is known as "North Island."

The wide public beaches were created during World War II when the bay was dredged to make

*Thomas A. Edison, inventor of the light bulb, personally supervised the installation of his incandescent lamps in the **Hotel del Coronado**. Edison pulled the switch on the hotel's first electrically lighted Christmas tree.*

It is said that writer L. Frank Baum patterned his Emerald City after the Del. He lived on Coronado and wrote several of the Oz books in the yellow house at 1101 Star Park Circle.

it deeper for the many large navy ships that anchored in the harbor. Ocean currents piled the sand up on the beach, where it remained.

The San Diego-Coronado Bay Bridge is more than two miles long. It's a toll bridge, so have some coins ready. Tiny **Bay View Park**, at the end of I Avenue and First Street, offers a great panoramic view of the bay. It's the place to go to take really terrific pictures of the bridge.

One of the first things you'll see on the "Island" is the red turrets of the **Hotel del Coronado**, known as "the Del." When the hotel opened in 1888, people came from all over the world to stay there. It's still an elegant and popular beach resort.

Spreckels Park, on Orange Avenue between 6th and 7th streets, offers Sunday band concerts at 6:00 p.m. (summer only). A great variety of bands are featured—from steel drums to navy brass. The lights of the harbor and the city are spectacular from the bridge at night.

Enough of city life? Take I-5 south for a visit to **Chula Vista Nature Interpretive Center**. Thousands of waterfowl and shorebirds flock to this salt marsh habitat. In spring, fleets of newly hatched ducklings may be seen sailing on open water. There are observation decks to view hawks and falcons that frequent the marsh, and there may be an occasional rare bird visitor from Mexico. You can touch the sandpapery skin of a friendly bat ray in the outdoor pool or look over the more than three hundred exhibits within the living wetland museum. Should you be in Chula Vista during the Christmas season, don't miss the decorations. The town goes all out to create a fantasyland of colorful lights.

A salt marsh is a low coastal grassland frequently overflowed by the tide. It's a breeding ground and nursery for many ocean fish and for water birds. The constant bath of nutrients carried in from the ocean is the basis of an important food chain. We must protect the remaining salt marshes from destruction, before further harm is done to the environment.

11. South of the Border and the Backcountry

Visiting a foreign country is always an adventure. If you're a citizen of the United States, you won't need a passport or a tourist card for a short visit to **Tijuana, Mexico**.

Take the San Diego trolley from downtown and walk across the border to avoid heavy traffic and long delays. Taxis are readily available and inexpensive in Tijuana. If you take a private vehicle into Mexico, be sure to tell your grown-up to get Mexican auto insurance. (This is not a trip for young people to do on their own. Go with a parent or other adult.) The **Cultural Center** is a great place to visit. All sorts of arts and crafts are on display, and the Omni Theater features a 45-minute film (in English, at 2:00 p.m. only) called *El Pueblo del Sol* (The City of the Sun). It shows historical places in Mexico. The wide screen makes you feel as though you are there. The museum is located in the Plaza Rio Tijuana.

Remember, you are a visitor. Mexican laws and rules of behavior are not the same as in the United States. And while many people speak English, it will be appreciated if you learn two Spanish words—*gracias* (thank you) and *por favor* (please).

"Montezuma's revenge" (diarrhea and nausea) afflicts many U.S. visitors to Mexico. Do not eat anything that is not cooked. Drink only bottled or canned juice and water. And remember, ice is frozen water.

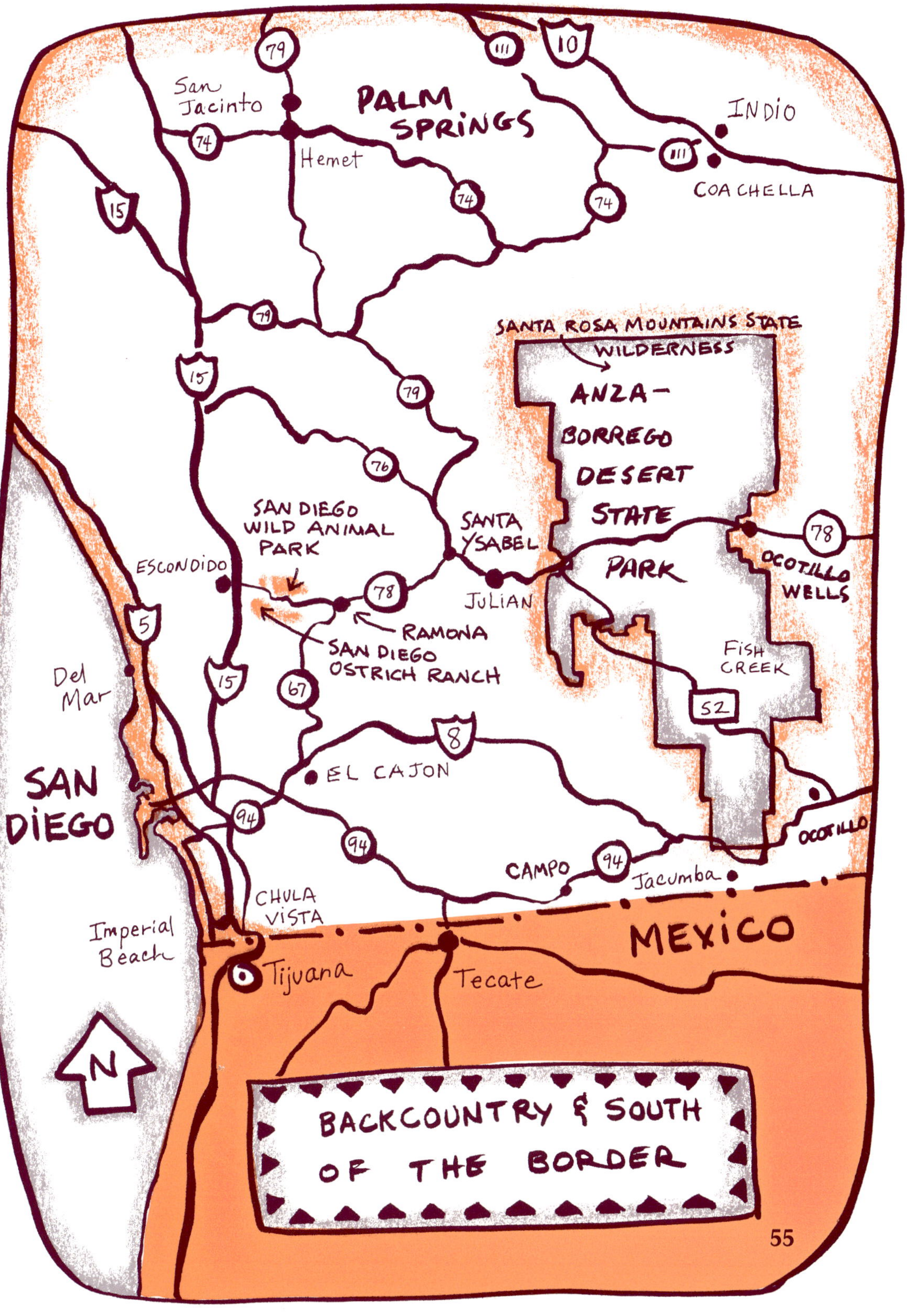
79
111
10
San Jacinto
PALM SPRINGS
INDIO
74
Hemet
111
COACHELLA
15
74
74
79
SANTA ROSA MOUNTAINS STATE WILDERNESS
15
79
ANZA-BORREGO DESERT STATE PARK
76
SAN DIEGO WILD ANIMAL PARK
SANTA YSABEL
78
ESCONDIDO
78
JULIAN
OCOTILLO WELLS
5
RAMONA
SAN DIEGO OSTRICH RANCH
Fish Creek
Del Mar
15
67
52
8
SAN DIEGO
EL CAJON
94
94
OCOTILLO
CAMPO
94
Jacumba
CHULA VISTA
MEXICO
Imperial Beach
Tijuana
Tecate
N
BACKCOUNTRY & SOUTH OF THE BORDER

Old No. 11, a 100-ton locomotive, ran for the Coos Bay Lumber Co. in 1929. She is now one of the restored iron horses at the **Campo Railway Museum**.

Ever listen to the lonesome wail of a train whistle and wonder what it would be like to ride the rails? Here is a chance to find out. Members of the **Pacific Southwest Railroad Museum** in **Campo** take restored steam or diesel locomotives out for a run through the backcountry every weekend. It's great fun to climb aboard one of these trains and with a whistle and a toot, chug into the past. Trains run Saturday and Sunday for a 16-mile one-hour trip. (Departure time may change according to the season.) You can also see locomotives and cars being restored to near-new condition at the museum.

In 1870, the **Washington Gold Mine** was named for our first president because the claim was staked on his birthday, February 22. I'll bet George would have been pleased about that.

The main room of the **Julian Pioneer Museum** was once a brewery, and then a blacksmith shop. The adobe walls were restored in 1952, and the fireplace is made of discarded Indian grinding stones.

Gold mines and boomtowns of the Old West seem very much alive when you step into the little mountain community of **Julian**. The best way to see the town is on foot. Many of the original buildings are still standing. The one-room Witch Creek School is next door to the Memorial Museum.

Just six blocks off the main street on Old Miners Trail, you can tour the hard rock **Eagle Mine**. After exploring the underground operations and seeing the milling process, don't miss the displays of mining machinery and tools of the 1870s as well as samples of gold-bearing quartz.

In the spring, the orchards are one big cloud of pink and white blossoms. In October, the town celebrates with "Apple Days." Harvest sheds and roadside stands overflowing with apples and jugs of sweet cider are awfully tempting. Don't be shy. Stop for a chat and a taste. Apple pie is a specialty of the restaurants any time of year.

Just west of Julian you'll find **Santa Ysabel**. Follow your nose to Dudley's Bakery for the yummiest breads, sweet rolls, and cookies in the country. There is a deli in the back where you can order sandwiches made with your choice of fresh bread. (Look over the barbed wire collection and some of the branding irons used by early Californians.)

A few miles farther east on State 78 will take you down the mountain and into the largest state park in the nation—**Anza-Borrego Desert**

State Park. Once you look past the dry, dusty shoulder of the highway, there is a whole world of fascinating plants, animals, and rock formations to explore.

Park headquarters is located in Borrego Springs. Large native palm trees shade the entrance, and the grounds are landscaped with strange-looking cactus and unusual desert plants. The Visitors Center is set partially underground, to insulate it from the desert heat. Two brass ram's heads are mounted on the double doors of the building. Pull the curling horns to open the doors. Inside there are interesting exhibits of desert life and a super slide program showing many of the animals and plants at different seasons of the year.

In the spring, a cactus wren may be singing from its nest in a teddy bear cholla right outside the Center's door. Pink chiffonlike blossoms cover the beaver tail plants. Don't pick them, though. They're protected by the Park Service and by the thousands of tiny glochids (hairlike stickers) that grow on the cactus pads.

There are miles of fabulous trails to hike or bike. You might even see bighorn sheep in Coyote Canyon or Palm Canyon. Several species of hummingbirds enjoy the desert flowers, and jet black phainopeplas (birds that resemble cardinals—except for the color) are common. You may hear the bubbling song of canyon wrens echoing down the slope or see a big desert jackrabbit lope off into the mesquite. The desert is a great place to explore (except in summer, when the temperature is often well over 100°F).

There are plenty of picnic spots and campgrounds in the park.

Better not hug the teddy bear cholla. Those are thorns, not fur, that make it look so cuddly.

It's fun to look for footprints in the desert sand. They may tell you a desert bighorn, a coyote, a covey of quail, or any of a dozen other animals have passed this way. Sometimes, by following footprints, you can find what the animal has been eating or maybe even find its home (don't disturb them, please).

Summertime rock temperatures are known to go as high as 190°F. Always carry plenty of water—and drink it! Dehydration is a serious problem. It's always a good idea to let someone know which trail you are taking and when you plan to return. And, of course, do not hike alone.

12. Memories

What was the most fun on your visit to San Diego? Lazy days at the beach? Surfing and sailing? Maybe it was Balboa Park and the zoo. Did you see the whales, explore a tide pool, or go to Mexico? Someone is sure to ask.

One of the nice things about travel is that you can enjoy the memories for a long time to come. Pictures and souvenirs help to keep the adventure fresh in your mind. When you see a travel program or read about San Diego, you can say, "I remember that. I was there." Perhaps you can even add interesting facts to a travel discussion.

Unpleasantries are learning experiences, too. Sometimes they make the best stories. Did you sit on a cactus or get sand in the picnic basket? No trip is complete without a few bloopers.

There are always little bonuses along the way, too, things you discover for yourself. You might develop a passion for Mexican food, or find an orange grove where you are invited to pick your own fruit. Keep your eyes and ears open: something awesome could be just around the corner.

There is no way you can see and do it all in just one trip. You may want to return to San Diego again and again. (Now you know why many people like to sing "California, Here I Come.")

Appendix

619 is the area code for all San Diego telephone numbers.

Anza-Borrego Desert State Park
About 100 miles east of San Diego
Park information, 767-4684

Balboa Park
Just north of downtown
From I-5 exit at Park Blvd.
Transit Bus #7
232-3821

Belmont Park
Mission Beach

Cabrillo National Monument
Tip of Point Loma, $3 per car or $1 per person by bus
Transit Bus #6, hourly
Handicapped access

Campland on the Bay
2211 Pacific Beach Dr.
San Diego, CA 92109
274-6260 for reservations

Catalina Island Seajet
696-0088 for information and reservations

Chula Vista Nature Interpretive Center
E Street exit off I-5 in Chula Vista, then west 1 block. Park in the Center's lot at the corner of E St. and Bay Blvd. A shuttle bus runs every 20 minutes to the Center. Charge for shuttle, admission to Center free.

Coronado
I-5 or Harbor Dr. to SR 75, which leads to the Bay Bridge toll gate

Ensenada Express
232-2109 for information

Farmers Bazaar
K St. and 7th Ave.
Open 7 days a week, 8:30 a.m. to 6:30 p.m.

Firehouse Museum
Corner of Columbia and Cedar sts.
Open Thursday through Sunday, 10:00 a.m. to 4:00 p.m.
Admission free
232-3473

Harbor Tours or Excursion
Harbor Drive at the foot of Broadway

Horton Plaza
Between Broadway and G sts. and First and Fourth aves.

Imperial House Restaurant's Mystery Café
505 Kalmia St. (downtown S.D.) or
Lake San Marcos Resort
Friday and Saturday
544-1600 for reservations

International Visitor Information Center
1st Ave. and F St., 11 Horton Plaza
San Diego, CA 92101
Open 8:30 a.m.-5:00 p.m. daily
236-1212

Julian
About 60 miles northeast of San Diego

Junior Theatre
239-1311 or 239-8355 for information

Junípero Serra Museum
Presidio Park
Closed Monday
Admission charge

La Jolla Caves
Coast Blvd. just off Prospect St. and La Jolla Blvd.
Transit Bus #34, admission charged

Marie Hitchcock Theatre
Palisades Building, Balboa Park
Shows at 11:00 a.m. and 1:00 and 2:00 p.m.
Saturday and Sunday

Maritime Museum
1306 N. Harbor Dr. at the foot of A St.

Mission Bay Visitors Information Center
2688 East Mission Bay Dr.
San Diego, CA 92109
9:00 a.m.-5:00 p.m. daily
276-8200

Mission San Diego de Alcala
East on I-8, then north on Mission Gorge Rd.,
   left on Twain Ave. (it becomes San Diego
   Mission Rd. after 1 block).
Donation

Marine Corps Recruit Depot Command Museum
225-3141 for visitor information
Free

Navy Ships Tour
Broadway Pier
Saturday and Sunday 1:00 p.m. to 4:00 p.m.
235-3534 for information
Free

Old Town
From I-5, exit at Old Town Ave.
From I-8, exit at Taylor St.

Old Town Trolley Tours
298-8687 for information

Old Town Park ranger-guided tour
2:00 p.m. daily from the Machado y Silvas Adobe
   across from the plaza

Pacific Southwest Railroad Museum
Campo, California
About 55 miles southeast of San Diego
697-7762 for information

The Plunge
Mission Beach
488-3110 for information

Prince and the Pauper Bookstore
3201 Adams Ave.

Reenactment of the Battle of San Pasqual
San Pasqual Battlefield State Park
Escondido
489-0076

Reuben H. Fleet Space Theater and Science Center
238-1168 for scheduled programs

San Diego Chargers (NFL)
Jack Murphy Stadium
August through December
280-2111 for information

San Diego Civic Theatre
236-6510 for information

San Diego County Fishing Piers:
Crystal Pier, Pacific Beach at the foot of Garnet St.
Imperial Beach Pier, at the foot of Elm St.
Oceanside Pier, Oceanside at the foot of 3rd St.
Shelter Island Pier, San Diego Bay
San Diego Public Fishing Pier, Ocean Beach
   at the foot of Niagara Street
No fees charged

San Diego Gulls
224-4171 for information

San Diego Ostrich Ranch
San Pasqual Rd. on the way to the Wild Animal
   Park
Escondido
Closed Tuesdays
Free

San Diego Padres (NL)
Jack Murphy Stadium
April through September
283-7294 for information

San Diego Park and Recreation Department
226-3407 for active sports information

San Diego Sockers (MISL)
San Diego Sports Arena
October through April
224-GOAL for information

San Diego Visitors Bureau
1200 Third Ave., Suite 824
San Diego, CA 92101
236-1212 weekdays

San Diego Wild Animal Park
I-15 north to Escondido
Open daily 9:00 a.m. to dusk
Handicapped access
234-6541

San Diego Zoo
Balboa Park
Open daily 9:00 a.m. to dusk
Handicapped access
234-3153

Scripps Institute of Oceanography
Just north of La Jolla on La Jolla Shores Dr.
Transit Buses #30 or #34
Suggested donation
Information 534-3474

Seaport Village
849 West Harbor Drive at Kettner Blvd.

Sea World
Mission Bay Park
Open 9:00 a.m. until dusk, winter
Mid-June until Labor Day, open until 11:00 p.m.
Handicapped access
TDD for the deaf
226-3901

Times Arts TIX Center
Horton Plaza
238-3810 for ticket information

Torrey Pines State Reserve
State 52 west to Ardath, turn north on Torrey
  Pines Rd.
$4 per car

Kidding Around with John Muir Publications

We are making the world more accessible for young travelers. In your hand you have one of several John Muir Publications guides written and designed especially for kids. We will be *Kidding Around* other cities also. Send us your thoughts, corrections, and suggestions. We also publish other young readers titles as well as adult books about travel and other subjects. Let us know if you would like one of our catalogs. All the titles below are 64 pages and $9.95, except for *Kidding Around the National Parks of the Southwest* and *Kidding Around Spain*, which are 108 pages and $12.95 each.

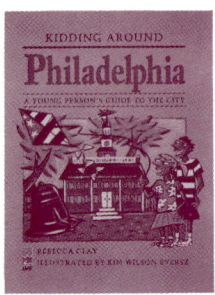

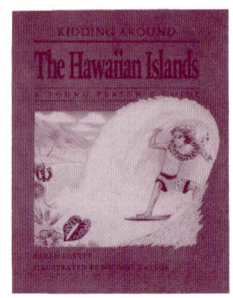

TITLES NOW AVAILABLE IN THE SERIES
Kidding Around Atlanta
Kidding Around Boston
Kidding Around Chicago
Kidding Around the Hawaiian Islands
Kidding Around London
Kidding Around Los Angeles
Kidding Around the National Parks of the Southwest
Kidding Around New York City
Kidding Around Paris
Kidding Around Philadelphia
Kidding Around San Diego
Kidding Around San Francisco
Kidding Around Santa Fe
Kidding Around Seattle
Kidding Around Spain
Kidding Around Washington, D.C.

Ordering Information
Your books will be sent to you via UPS (for U.S. destinations). UPS will not deliver to a P.O. Box; please give us a street address. Include $2.75 for the first item ordered and $.50 for each additional item to cover shipping and handling costs. For airmail within the U.S., enclose $4.00. All foreign orders will be shipped surface rate; please enclose $3.00 for the first item and $1.00 for each additional item. Please inquire about foreign airmail rates.

Method of Payment
Your order may be paid by check, money order, or credit card. We cannot be responsible for cash sent through the mail. All payments must be made in U.S. dollars drawn on a U.S. bank. Canadian postal money orders in U.S. dollars are acceptable. For VISA, MasterCard, or American Express orders, include your card number, expiration date, and your signature, or call (800) 888-7504. Books ordered on American Express cards can be shipped only to the billing address of the cardholder. Sorry, no C.O.D.'s. Residents of sunny New Mexico, add 5.875% tax to the total.

Address all orders and inquiries to:
John Muir Publications
P.O. Box 613
Santa Fe, NM 87504
(505) 982-4078
(800) 888-7504